ANDERS INVESTIGATIONS

TAMING THE *Grumpy* BODYGUARD

WILLA DREW
&
A. MIRACLE

Moving Words Publishing

Published by: Moving Words Publishing

www.movingwordspublishing.com

Copyright © 2025 by **Willa Drew** & **A. Miracle**

Cover Art: Cupcake_Cat1235

Cover & Interior Design: A Fabulous Production

www.afabulousproduction.com

Paperback: 978-1-957897-26-4

First Edition: November 2025

CONTENTS

To the IRL Pablo

ONE

BODYGUARD

AT TEN IN THE evening, the office of Anders Investigations is finally quiet. Blissfully quiet.

Owning my own private security business in Los Angeles has been a dream of mine for a decade. Nine months into the enterprise, I have a small storefront in Westwood, an assistant who isn't taking time off for auditions, and a full roster of clients. After years of living *eight* to a barrack in the Marines followed by shared quarters with my fellow bodyguards at my first boss's mansion, having a place that has my name on it is all the proof I need that my solitary lifestyle is paying off.

Across the room, the coffee pot hisses as if reprimanding me.

"I don't need company," I grumble to the machine.

With a new business, I don't have time for people. Not unless you count the potential bodyguards I've interviewed. I can't do everything on my own. I'm not Superman.

Yet.

A soft yet grating noise pulls at my attention. Is that scratching? Is there some kind of vermin in the walls seeking shelter from an unusual-for-LA bout of November rain?

I take a sip of my coffee and wince. The bitter brew is colder than the drizzle outside. I pull up the schematics on the house of the client, who likes her privacy as much as I do, and scan the perimeter of the property for ways intruders can enter.

The scuffing noise invades my thoughts again, louder this time and definitely not coming from the walls but from the back door. The hairs on the back of my neck rise. My bodyguard mode activated, I sift through the possible worst-case scenarios.

Is someone trying to jimmy the lock? Break in?

If they think they're stealing from me, they have a hard lesson coming their way.

I push back my chair, make sure my handgun is secure in my holster, snatch up the baseball bat I keep in the closet, and creep out of my office to investigate.

Orange light from the streetlamp offers little illumination through the window that faces the back parking lot, but I keep the inside light off. My jaw clenches. I'll catch these thieves by surprise. Another scuffling noise, and the back door jiggles. With a quick twist of the knob, I fling the door open and swing at head height.

The bat flies through the empty air as something wet bumps against my leg. I spin to catch a blur of black speeding down the hallway.

"Hey … you …" I bang the door shut and tear after the creature. If it's a rat, it's exceptionally large. Maybe the most impressive rat in LA.

Nails scrape against my hardwood floors as the animal makes the turn. I surge forward, my legs pumping. Whatever it is, it's quick. The black, spiky furball heads for my office, and I lunge at the form. My stomach slams against the hardwood, but I come up empty-handed.

From under my desk, two eyes stare at me. Mismatched eyes: one shocking blue, the other brown. They accompany a long snout covered in grimy, wiry hair. I grunt, and two large triangle ears perk up.

"Hello, Dog." At my utterance, the animal's head twists a fraction to the left like it's a scientist studying a new species.

The dog tilts its head as if thinking and doesn't take his stare off me. No growling. No baring teeth, just quiet curiosity, as if I, not he, am out of place. My heart beats faster.

"Where did you come from?" Right. Dogs don't talk. So he... or is it a she? . . . is not about to answer.

I hold my breath and carefully stretch out my arm. "You can't stay under there."

My hand grazes rough fur, but the dog, like a loaded spring, charges past me. I do a burpee to get up to my feet and give chase. Again. The tiny intruder ricochets around my office like he's in a pinball machine, scraping by the reception desk, overturning a chair in the waiting room, and bumping into the Ficus. Soil spills out of the potted plant. Next in the path of the creature's wrath is the trash can that doesn't stand a chance against the tiny menace.

I curse at the dog, who is surprisingly nimble in this small space. Something I am not. But I know the layout, and if I keep corralling it forward, there'll be only one place the dog can end up. The animal zips into the bathroom, and I slam the door shut. Perfect. Thankfully, my Major won't ever find out that his training was used to detain a tiny dog, not an enemy combatant.

Sweat trickles down my temple. My Marines training did *not* teach me what to do with a captured stray dog. I brush my hand over the freshly cropped hair on my head and pace the hallway. What do I do? I hear the dog moving around on the other side of the door.

I growl at the ceiling.

Yep. I can't solve this by myself.

I slide my phone out of my pocket.

This is what I'm going to have to do.

I pull up my assistant's number and type up a message.

Me: There's a stray dog in our bathroom.

My phone comes to life. Gretchen's smiling face urges me to pick up.

I hit answer. "Hi—"

"Is the door stuck again?" My assistant's actual face, with a halo of long gray hair, dominates the screen. She's great with technology, especially for someone from my parents' generation, but she always gets too close to the screen when she's not wearing her glasses. "The super promised he fixed the sticky handle."

"He did. I locked the dog in."

The phone swings away as I watch the photos in Gretchen's apartment swoosh by. The movement stops, and her face reappears. "Are you afraid of it?"

"No." I bark out. As if.

"How big is the dog?" Gretchen's nose crinkles as she rests the phone somewhere on her desk.

"Small." I cough. "Tiny."

Gretchen's eyebrows shoot up, but she schools her face back to the pleasant neutral position she welcomes my clients with. Her mouth opens, closes, then opens again.

Somehow, I just know I'm not going to like what she says next.

Two

Dog

Coming to Dad's office was as far as I got in my planning. I know five different ways to get here from our apartment and a sixth that no one else knows about.

The automatic lights come on, and my chest expands. I look around the bathroom: sink, poop pot, shelves—it's mostly the same, but maybe less gross. A girl must have been in here last because the poop pot is thankfully closed.

My stomach gurgles, and the fried chicken I found behind the gas station threatens to re-enter this world. I gag. Beast's footsteps on the other side of the closed door are nothing like Dad's. Why isn't Dad coming? I shiver at the thought of being alone. If he's not here, where else could he be?

I need a new plan.

I hop onto the lowest shelf and sniff the glass that smells like lemons. You should see the bathroom we have at home. So gross.

Hmm, what's that other smell? Something... familiar. I sniff deeper. My nose twitches, trying to place it. *My bone.* Oh, how I've missed my baby girl. My tail pops up as I follow the scent.

Dad and I have spent a lot of time in this room. For a while, I thought sitting on the poop pot was his job. Hiding my bone here was the only thing that got me through those smelly days.

"That coffee goes right through me," Dad would say.

I never did understand the point of drinking that black stuff if it just comes right back out. Seems like a waste of time to me.

The shelves are still stacked with the magazines Dad would flip through whenever we got comfortable in here. I'm a dog, so I understand finding the perfect poop spot is hard. Dad reusing the same one is pretty gross if you ask me. But hey, who am I to judge? My favorite hobby involves scootching my butt on the carpet when I think no one is watching.

Dad said my bone was the secret to me being the goodest boy. I've seen those doomsday prepper shows. You never know when you might be locked in the bathroom with someone searching for the golden poop moment. You might as well have a snack.

Am I right?

Nose to the ground, I get back to business.

"Don't worry, baby girl, I'll find you," I woof, hoping my bone hears me. I was made for this.

Sniffing out where things are is something I'm never wrong about. This nose is made of gold.

I jump up on the poop pot and from there onto a higher shelf. I sniff every corner, knocking off everything in my way because this is an emergency. A bone emergency. Leaving no spot un-sniffed, I balance on the front of the sink. The scent grows stronger. I must be getting closer.

In the large glass thing that hangs on the wall, a mud-caked dog stares back at me. Not the internet-famous marine working dog who everyone knows and loves. Is that what I look like now? You can't even see my gray eyebrows. My eyes widen. What if I smell as bad as I look? I'm all for a nice earthworm perfume on a summer day but even I have standards. I want the ladies to walk past me in the park and think, "Wow, now this is a guy I want to share my bone with."

Personally, I'm an Aveeno Oatmeal Shampoo kind of guy. I take a whiff. I do smell worse than I look. I reek. My tail tucks between my legs. Dad always made me look and smell good before we went bye-bye to the park or the office. After each bath, he would tell me how handsome of a boy I was. I always shook and shivered while secretly enjoying it. A small whimper leaves me. I miss you, Dad. I even miss our bathtime. I hope I find you soon. Skin shuddering under my fur, I remind myself of the tasks at hand.

Find bone. Find Dad. Take nap. In that order.

Sorry, Dad. Priorities.

I walk to the edge of the sink and look down at the last un-sniffed corner. There behind a broom is my bone. She's waiting for me. I hope she missed me as much as I missed her. My mouth starts to water. Man, even after the gas station chicken incident, I can't say no to my bone. I jump down, paw it out of its little nook, and sit on the floor.

Task number one is complete. Go me. My tail wags. I really am a good boy.

Human voices sound from behind the bathroom door, and the magic ball on the door rattles.

Oh, no.

Hide.

Where do I hide?

As the door creaks, my heart is no longer in my body. I mean, I'm small. I can fit in most places. But where are the stacks of empty pizza boxes Dad hoarded that were tall enough for me to hide behind? The rumbling in my stomach returns. To cover my bone, I lay down. I slip into work mode and stay as still as possible like I did when danger was close by.

Beast slowly opens the door like I'm the suspicious one here, and his gaze finds me. He's real tall. And . . . wide. The sleeves of his suit strain against his massive muscles. In his hand is one of those black rectangular soul-catching devices my dad loved putting in my face. I dare not breathe.

Be a statue. Don't blink.

My eyes strain as they dry like they do when I stick my head out the window for too long. If I keep them open for much longer, I may fart and puke at the same time.

Luckily, the door closes as quickly as it opened and I unfreeze. I stand up and blink. My legs wobble. Tiny shivers run up my spine. I lay back down, giving my body the much-needed rest from that large test of strength. My heart returns to my chest. I used to be able to hold the pose for a lot longer when I was working, but the pizza nights with Dad have made it much harder.

"So cute." A woman's voice says from behind the closed door. "Is it hungry?"

"We didn't exactly have a conversation."

Now that I can breathe again, I get into my prime bone-munching position, wrapping my paws around my girl. Yeah, this feels right. I give her one slow lick to take in the taste of the life I used to know. Bones are all I need.

Oh yeah, and Dad.

"Do you have any meat?" says the mystery woman.

My ears perk up. I might like her. I could go for some meat. Knowing that a chance for chicken nuggets or a cheeseburger is a possibility, I put my bone back in the corner for safekeeping. I return to the door, sitting in my pretty boy position with my legs swept to the side, and wait for it to open.

Something other than me growls on the other side of the door, and I go from pretty boy to dangerous boy in .5 seconds. I back up and give a low growl as a warning not to mess with me.

"No." Beast grumbles.

Oh. No meat? That's . . .um . . . disappointing.

The noise on the other side of the door intensifies. I extend my ears to hear what all the hubbub is about, but the sound moves away. I shift a bit closer.

I hear the word "Dog."

I'm a dog.

"Treats."

I like treats.

"Toys."

I really like toys.

"Vet."

Nope, don't like that.

THREE

BODYGUARD

The pacing in front of the bathroom isn't helping my heart rate. I stop. The accompaniment of claws clacking on the bathroom floor on the other side of the door stops as well. I add the phone number of the local animal control services to my contacts and go back to reading the article on what to do if you find a stray dog. There aren't any links on what to do if said dog gets inside your office. I resume my pacing, and the dog resumes his.

The front door flies open, and Gretchen rushes in with more bags than I thought possible to carry in two hands.

"Is he still here?" She looks around the office as if I would let that little creature out of the bathroom to muddy up Anders Investigations. "Where is he?"

"Bathroom." I point my thumb to where I've detained the enemy.

Gretchen drops the bags and almost runs past me. "How friendly is he? Did you pet him?"

"The article advised not to. He might have rabies."

"I didn't see him foaming at the mouth in the photo. He's probably just lost. Poor baby." Gretchen twists the handle and peeks inside. The dog attempts to squeeze through the opening. "Hello, sweetie. Look at his eyes." Gretchen squeals and crouches in front of the dog whose breed I can't even identify.

"It's called heterochromia." Yeah, I googled that too.

"They're so striking." Gretchen motions to the bags in the middle of the reception area. "I wasn't sure how old he was, so the clerk at the pet store suggested several kinds of kibble."

A bark redirects our attention to the reason my night went awry. The dog, clearly satisfied that the attention is back on it, smiles. I've heard that dogs can smile, but seeing his muzzle stretch in a grin, his eyes sparkling, I question my original assessment.

"Food? Do you want food?" Gretchen rises and fishes out one bag. "This says for small dogs under thirty-five pounds. Do you think he is under that?"

He doesn't look much bigger than a loaf of bread. "I have not picked it up."

"I think he is small enough." Gretchen stalks into the kitchenette and pulls two of my extra-wide jumbo mugs from Blend, my favorite local coffee shop. She pours the kibble into the red one that I usually use for my late-night cereal snack and sets it in front of the dog's face.

Fully out of the bathroom, the dog sniffs the offering and tries the piled-high round brown balls. With a bark of approval, he plunges his muzzle into the food and crunches on the rapidly disappearing chow.

Gretchen fills the other bowl with water and places it next to the food. The dog's small body is now entirely on display, which means I can tell he's actually a boy and is not neutered. He takes Gretchen's offering and slurps like he hasn't had a drop of liquid in days.

"Are you lost, little guy?" Gretchen unpacks the collection of bags while the dog's tail wags a mile a minute, painting an even bigger grin on her face.

Did the dog put a spell on my assistant already? It's been 2.5 seconds. If he thinks that's going to get it out of going to Animal Control, he's got another think coming. Sugar might be my weak spot, but small things like dogs and children are most definitely not.

The middle of my reception is now a pile that includes a dog bed, a plastic mat that apparently goes under the food and water bowls, a pack of bright neon-green tennis balls, a collar and a harness, a leash, smaller bags with dog treats, and a roll of poop bags.

Poop bags in the middle of my place of business is not what I imagined this work would entail. Blood and gore? Yes. Stalkers? Absolutely. Angry spouses? Comes with the job. Poop bags? No way.

"I asked you to get something to tie the dog over till morning." I give her my signature stare. Usually, the less I say, the more people talk. They talk themselves into whatever I need them to say or do.

"You said, and I quote: use the business card to keep the dog alive." Gretchen pulls out her phone. "I called the shelter, and it's currently full, which means they can't keep him there for long if the owner is not found quickly, but. . ."

She hesitates. "They do have a shelter-at-home initiative."

"Great. And . . ." I gesture to the bags.

"Because, as a good Samaritan, you might need to keep the dog for up to thirty days." She hands me a pack of treats and a tennis ball.

I half-choke in astonishment. "Me?"

Shelter at home? Like my home? Absolutely not. I'm not the dog-dad type.

"You take him." I hand the tennis ball back to Gretchen.

"My apartment doesn't allow dogs. And I'm here five days a week or more. I'll take care of him when I'm in the office. All you have to do is feed and walk him at night." She presses the ball into my palm.

"This is a place of business, not a charity." I re-approach the animal and cross my arms. The dog stops drinking as his different-colored eyes peer into my soul. He goes back to smiling. It seems every time I say the word dog, his attention returns to me.

"Only for thirty days or until the owner is found." Gretchen trails behind. "I'll make up posters with his picture and place them around here and online. I'll even take him to the vet."

I bend and reach for the small black body, but he inches away. I step forward. He steps back. His smile grows wider. I ball my fists.

"This is not a game," I say.

His ears perk up, and his tail wags as he retreats and switches to a run. I groan at the ceiling. The dog is fast for having such short legs. I chase him around the reception area, to the bathroom door, to the back door, and back to the pile of dog stuff. If I took him on my morning runs, I might actually improve my personal record. I stop and give the dog the stare I gave Gretchen minutes ago.

The dog makes a sound. Not a bark, more like a hacking cough. A stream of undigested dog food and something green, peppered with unidentifiable chunks comes out of his little mouth. It's like watching a clown car. How can such a tiny dog throw up so much?

"He could be sick if he's been out too long in this cold rain." Gretchen runs over and hovers over a mountain of dog upchuck–another pile I never expected in my office.

Gretchen claps her palms on her thighs, trying to entice the dog to come to her. "Komm hier."

I recognize that she's speaking in her native German.

The dog runs over to her as if on command.

"What did you just say?" I ask.

"Come here." She looks at the dog. "Come here, little guy." Her words in English don't have any effect on the dog. On the contrary, he backs away from her.

"Say it in German."

"Why?"

"Just do it." I squeeze the tennis ball.

"Komm heir."

The dog stops. His full attention is back on Gretchen.

"I think he understands commands in German. I know K9 units train their dogs in German sometimes." I crouch down to the dog's level. "Say something else. Like, sit or roll over."

"Sitz," says Gretchen.

The dog sits. My excitement grows.

"Rolle," she says, and the dog rolls over.

"Lauf."

The dog starts running.

"Is he like a super smart dog?" I ask.

"He's definitely trained." Gretchen side-eyes me. Which will make it so much easier for you to keep him until his owner shows up."

I glare at her, but she has her attention on the dog. "Komm."

The dog comes to Gretchen.

"Bleib."

This time, when I approach the dog, he does not move. Gretchen smiles at me. The *dog* smiles at me.

I point a finger at my assistant. "You're on dog-sitting duty. And on finding the dog's owner duty. Shelter is the only thing I'm providing."

Both smile wider.

I shove my hands into my pockets. It better be less than thirty days.

I need my peace and quiet.

Four

Dog

Turns out that Beast isn't too bad.

After we finish playing a rousing game of tag in Dad's office, I have to sit down and take a break. I can't help it. These little legs wear out fast at my age. The nice lady who smelled like flowers bolted, leaving just us men. Beast seems a little grumpy, but I'm used to working with men like that. All business, no play. A little time with me will fix him right up. I guess I might as well help him out while I wait for Dad to come back.

Did you see all that stuff the lady bought for me? They must be rich. I respect it. What I didn't expect was her talking in my work language. Before Dad and I retired, I was a lean, mean working machine. He was the best military police dog handler in the Marine Corps and made me the best at tracking and finding things. That's why I'm sure I can find Dad and also why I've never lost a bone.

Mental note: Go check on my girl in the bathroom.

I still remember everything he taught me. He would have me sniff a cloth, and then I'd have to go find a similar item. Ah, those were fun days. The things I discovered that led to all the good boy belly rubs. A pang of sadness hits my chest. Is Dad okay?

"You're looking a little rough, aren't you, Dog?" Beast crouches down onto one knee.

"That is *not* my name." I squint with no head tilt, which says I mean business.

"And we are back to barking." He pulls the flat black device out of his pocket and studies it. "Here it is." He clears his throat. "Ruhig."

That command means quiet, so I stop. I can be quiet because I'm a good boy. He'll see.

"You really are quite smart." Beast walks over to a plastic bag and grabs something.

The shakes of excitement ripple along my fur. A new bone? A new ball? Oh, maybe it's a new treat!

"The least I can do is get you cleaned up." He faces me.

Well, that's none of those. There's a fluffy white thing in his hands. Major letdown. Why does he have a towel? Dad only brings out the towel when he spills his beer or . . .

Oh, no.

Not a bath. It's not possible, not here. There's not even a torture tub here. Beast reaches down and picks me up like I'm a sack of potatoes. Curse these tiny legs. This grumpy stranger might be dressed like Dad and work at Dad's office, but he is *not* my dad. And I've reached my limit. Bath time is a special thing to share with someone. I don't even know this guy. When he holds me against him, his stomach is hard like the floor he just stole me from. He clearly doesn't have a nightly toasted fluffernutter before bed.

I wriggle in a last attempt to get free, but his boulders for arms squeeze tighter, almost popping my head off. I give in and take a good look at the office from so high since Beast is much taller than Dad.

Why was he sitting where Dad sat? Puzzled, I watch him pick up a tiny sweater on an even tinier hanger off his squeaky-clean desk. Not a paper or cheeseburger wrapper in sight.

Beast walks us up a flight of stairs into a small apartment I've never been to and goes straight into a bigger bathroom, where he seals us inside and turns on the water faucet for the sink.

"Let's get you clean and put . . . whatever this is"—he yanks the sweater off the hanger—"on you. Gretchen thinks if you look cute, there's more of a chance that people will send your photo around, and your owner will find you."

I'm not wearing that.

Dad never ever *ever* makes me wear anything fuzzy. This ridiculousness has sparkly stones. You've got to be kidding me. Who am I? A fashionista? Absolutely not. The last thing I wore was a service dog vest before my retirement. Ever since *that*, Dad has only used my favorite harness.

I pull my ears to my head. There is no actual way he would make me wear that, right? I stare at the man then at the sweater. He can wear it if he likes it so much.

"Hope this is safe for dogs." Beast pours a stream of something clear into the filling sink, and my nose twitches at the familiar scent. Dad smells like this after he takes his showers.

I wiggle in his arms, my paws skimming the surface of the sudsy water, then spread my legs wide to teeter on the porcelain edges. My plan works for all of three seconds, but one paw slips and sinks into the water. I yelp. Bubbles and water spray around the room like wet confetti, and I scramble up Beast's broad chest, over his shoulder, and down the other side.

He does a poor job of shaking off the excess water and swears like I haven't heard since Dad left the Marines.

Beast tugs at the hem of his shirt. "I didn't sign up for this."

Join the club.

He makes that low growling noise again and strips off the drenched shirt. I gawk at his lack of hair. What is it with these humans? Do they have something against fur? Aren't they cold? This one has hard ridges across his stomach. To my surprise, he peels off his pants as well. I shut my eyes, not wanting to see if he takes off anything more. There are limits, and we just met. Shouldn't he take me out first?

"There. Happy? Now we're both having a bath."

Strong fingers grip my torso, and my eyes can't resist.

Ah, so he's a briefs guy. Interesting.

I'm tucked into his hairless chest as he walks past the sink and steps into the shower. He twists a knob, and cold water douses me.

I didn't want it to be like this, but now I must do it.

I'll be peeing in his most expensive shoes as soon as he goes to sleep.

Five

BODYGUARD

AFTER MY SECOND SHOWER of the day, I shrug on my favorite Marines Get It Done sweatshirt and walk down the stairs. Dog pads behind me, giving me a "really?" attitude. The puffy green sweater I wrangled onto him is not quite the same color as mine, but we might be matching a bit too much. My office is the only room with a light still on. Working past midnight is not new for me but taking pictures of a dog in a bejeweled *Pawliday Love* sweater in my office is a first.

Hopefully a last as well.

I send them to Gretchen, and my phone immediately dings.

Gretchen: He looks so much better. Like a proper little dog.

Me: Smells better, too.

Gretchen: Don't forget to take him out for his business before you turn in for the night.

Yes, Mom. I shudder. My assistant might be my mom's age, but she's the polar opposite of my mother. Gretchen moved here to be closer to her daughter whereas I rarely knew where my mom was.

With a sigh, I stab out a "will do," shove my phone away, and get back to the work that pays the bills.

Security threats don't assess themselves. I enlarge the plans for next week's venue where my client is performing. Four exits means doubling the projected number of my people. Dog pitter-patters over to my chair with a low woof, which seems to be his way of announcing his presence.

"Hello to you, too," I say.

Dog sniffs my shoes, then my ankles, and gives another woof.

"What now?"

Dog whimpers at me, hunkers down, lays his small head over his paws, and digs his ocean blue and brown eye into my soul. "Damn, you're good."

I open a treat bag that's migrated onto my desk from Dog's pile of stuff Gretchen put on my credit card. It's not like my accountant will accept dog treats as a business expense.

I drop a small bone-shaped biscuit without making eye contact. The crunching takes less than three seconds. Then a bark. I think it's a happy bark. Am I able to hear the difference in his barks now? That can't be. I'm getting soft. I glance down. Dog barks again while smiling and wagging his tail and exits the office.

Multitasker.

I force my gaze back to the computer screen. The venue. Four exits. What was I supposed to do here? With a quieter woof, the dog re-enters the office, the green tennis ball in his mouth. He circles himself once, twice, and then he lies down so close to my feet that I can feel his fur through my socks. Ball nestled between his body and paws like a security blanket, the dog rests his muzzle on the top of my shoe. His tail taps against the floor under my desk. It's not as quiet in here as I'd like it to be, but I can work.

Another happy bark comes from under my desk. Warmth from the small body that's now covering both of my shoes seeps through the leather and travels all the way to my chest. I catch a corner of my lip sliding up and school it back to its usual, neutral setting. This arrangement is only temporary. Thirty days tops, I remind myself. Surely, with how cute and well-trained he is, his owner will show up soon. Probably tomorrow.

Tonight, I need to finish my assessment.

Dog's nose leaves my foot and sniffs around. He becomes a small bulldozer, shoving at my feet as his paws scrape the floor.

"What's going on now? Is there a rat in the basement?" I've never been down there, but the way the office is positioned, there's clearly one beneath, at least on one side.

Dog's scratching intensifies.

Cursing under my breath, I slide off my chair, get onto my knees, and pocket the loose tennis ball. I swipe the dog out of the way to see what he's pawing at. Is there actually something there? I rise and shove my desk aside. Without it covering the floor, I see that there's a slightly larger gap between some of the boards.

"What did you find here?" I run my fingers along the space. The shape and size of it forms a square. I push on the unusual part of the floor, and with a soft pop, one side springs up to reveal a handle.

The dog barks and looks at me as if encouraging me to pull. I should consult the plans of the building. I tap my foot. Dog's tail wags. The buzz of curiosity in my skull takes over. I do what I wouldn't advise any of my clients.

I yank on the handle.

The trap door opens, and a ladder with worn-out steps disappears into pitch black. I move my hand around the perimeter of the opening, looking for a light switch. When I find none, I take out my phone and turn on the flash-light. Dog peers into the darkness with me, its head bent low. Our breaths come quickly. Is it a rat? An intruder. A secret room? Ready for anything, we look at each other and back at the murky opening. Nothing moves below.

Dog paws at the edge.

"You stay here. Mystery basement isn't a place for someone as tiny as you."

I test the first rung of the ladder. The next. Nothing creaks or moves. The muscles in my shoulders tighten. I take one more step down when the dog lurches. My heart plummets. He's too fast. I teeter on the rung as I reach for Dog.

Dropping my phone, I catch the falling animal. Somewhere below, my phone clatters.

"What are you doing?" My voice shakes more than my hands. I clutch the dog to my chest and finish my descent. "You've no idea how deep this is."

My shoes hit solid concrete. I take a long breath in and out. The cool basement is not much more than six feet tall, because my head is practically scraping the ceiling. Holding the dog in one arm like a football, I retrieve my phone to shine the flashlight. Not a room. A hallway. With only one path to follow, I make my way down the corridor covered in unpainted drywall. A couple of turns, and I face a dead end with another ladder.

Dog leaps out of my arms and onto the ladder as if he knows what to do. He paws at the bottom of the door, which is pretty scratched up. He woofs.

"Someone's impatient. Ruhig." I say the one command I've memorized.

Instead of getting quiet, Dog repeats his bark, demanding I open the door.

German was supposed to get Dog to do what I wanted. So far, his woofs are better at making me do what he wants.

One more bark.

"Fine." I jiggle the handle, find the lock in the deadbolt, and push the door up.

Dog rushes out.

I scale the rungs of the ladder as fast as possible. My head pops up to an area surrounded by shrubbery. The tiny creature probably found his way through the bottom, but I have to carefully push the leaves to the side to find my way out.

Out to the park that's across the street from my office.

It's the middle of the night, and the couple of lights along the walkway that cut through the grassy area cast an eerie glow. The only living creature I see around is Dog, who runs over to a bench and lifts his leg. Nothing comes out, but that doesn't stop him from going to the trash can next to it and lifting his leg once more. Nothing again. He circles the trash can and runs over to the nearest tree. Leg up. Now, something comes out.

"Komm." I try another command.

He returns to me. I turn to go, but he beelines to another tree, sniffs it, and cocks his leg. The little guy proceeds to mark the territory tree by tree as if he's greeting old friends. By the fifth tree, the dog lifts his leg, and nothing happens. This doesn't seem to deter him from continuing. My lips stretch into a smile. This dog is something else. Or are all dogs this funny?

Six

Dog

THIS PARK IS MY favorite place ever. Dad and I used to come here at least a couple of times a week. We would walk the same path, and I would pee on the same trees every time. These trees were mine, marked with my scent (and pee), and every other dog that comes in here knows it.

Finishing my routine of marking my territory, I make my way back over to the beast to make sure he is also aware that this is my park.

"Komm. Fuss." The familiar commands tug at my heart. Dad's been the only person to use them. I walk back to Beast a bit slower, letting the memories of Dad play out.

"I know, I know, don't judge me. I'll eat better starting Monday," Dad would say to me. By Tuesday, we were ordering pizza.

I jump up on the bench we would sit on while he tried to catch his breath during our walk. When will Dad be back? I'm not giving up. I know he'd never give up on me. I survey the park again. No Dad. Another place to mark off my "Where's-Dad?" search list.

Beast calls for me again. I gotta hand it to him, the sweater is pretty cozy, but I'll deny it if anyone asks. Maybe he's not so bad? He does seem pretty helpful. And, okay, the whole bath thing was not as dramatic as I made it look. I *am* clean, I guess. Dad would've wanted me to be clean before going to the park. And Beast did keep me from going splat in the basement. I lift my head. What if I ask him to help me find

Dad? My heart beats a little faster at the idea. I scramble off the bench and run back toward Beast, barking a friendly "hello."

I smile.

Beast's lips stretch, but he doesn't show his teeth. He is so close to giving me a cheesy grin, I can feel it. I knew I would be able to help him. I hope he helps me, too. I wag my tail harder and give him my biggest bark.

Finally, for the first time today, I see his teeth as he pulls a round disk from behind his back. Wow, that was quick. Go me!

"Do you know how to fetch, Dog?" Beast flings the disc, and it goes flying across the grass. I look between him and where it landed. Tilting my head, I yip to explain that I'm a tennis ball kind of dog, not a flying disc dog. What do I look like? A cat?

Beast chuckles. "No? How about this?" He reaches into his pocket and pulls out the green tennis ball. My green tennis ball.

As my body shakes, I let my excited barks out.

New Plan. Ball. Bone. Dad. Nap.

Beast rears back and throws the ball. I take off at full speed, following the bright blur through the air to where it lands in the grass by the bushes. Maybe Beast and I are friends. Once he finds Dad, we can all come to the park. Yeah, I like that plan.

I pick up the ball and drop my friendship offering in front of Beast.

"Real friends throw balls for their friends," I bark.

He throws it, and a full laugh comes out of his chest. It must feel as good as a big bark feels for me. I smile at Beast, turn, and take off.

"What a good boy," rings through the night air behind me.

Seven

BODYGUARD

SOMETHING COOL PRESSES AGAINST my bicep. Can't be snow. It's December but I'm in LA. Am I bleeding? I pry open my eyes and glance at my arm.

Dog stares back at me, his nose nuzzled against my skin. Is he grinning? His small head plunks onto my bare chest, and his stubby legs bunch up the bed sheets until his warm body is flush against my torso.

It's been this way for almost a month. Tingles travel down my spine. Is my bed that much more comfortable than the dog bed Gretchen bought?

"Morning, Dog." I scratch behind his left ear, and the *thump, thump, thump* of his little heart shifts into overdrive. I retrieve Dog's favorite toy–the tennis ball which I use whenever I need to get him moving–and throw it across the room. Dog lunges off the bed in pursuit.

"I suppose you need a walk."

The dog jumps up and down in place.

"Guess that's a yes." I slide off the bed, take care of my own bathroom business, and pull on joggers and a hoodie. By the door, I tie my laces and attach the long lead to a harness I bought on my rounds yesterday. I snap the clasp shut and tap his head. "Tartan is way more manly than that sparkly shit Gretchen got you."

I swear I get a "you know it" grin from him.

We take the normal route to the park this morning. No tunnels today. It's still early, so the workday crowd isn't around yet. First, Dog climbs onto the bench and looks over the park from his higher ground, which I've learned is his usual. He jumps off and circles the area by the eucalyptus tree.

"Ready for a run?" I ask. The commands in German work ninety percent of the time, but I swear he also understands English.

Dog leaps up and down, which I take as a yes.

My concern that Dog wouldn't be able to keep up this time melts away as my feet pound the pavement. Like all other mornings, he zooms alongside me like he's a tiny super-dog flying along the path. I smile. I'm definitely looking online to see if they have doggy Superman costumes for Halloween. We could go as twins.

After my mandatory three laps around the park, we head back to the office. The door to the reception room is open. Dog trots through and gives Gretchen his good morning bark.

"Morning, Boss," she says as I enter the reception area. Gretchen grins at Dog. "And boss #2."

Dog shoots across the room to his corner and laps water from his bowl.

The phone on Gretchen's desk rings. "Hello. Yes. Hold on." She pushes the speaker phone button. "You still there?"

"Yeah, hello. I saw your online post. Do you have my dog?"

My throat goes dry.

"Yes," says Gretchen.

Dog leans against my leg.

"Great. I've been so worried about Rocko. I'm in Westwood. Are you nearby?"

Dog does not look like a Rocko, I think to myself.

I grip the edge of Gretchen's desk and avoid looking at him.

Gretchen arranges a meeting with Dog's owner at Blend, the closest coffee shop in the area, and ends the call. I suck in a breath. Why do my lungs hurt? The air conditioner has been off for a month.

"You okay?" Gretchen's hand is on my forearm.

I clear my throat to dislodge a boulder that's clogging it. "It's good news. Dog's place is with his owner."

"Oh, sweetie. I'm sorry. I know you liked having the dog around."

"You want me to pick you up a coffee?" I scratch my eye.

"No." Gretchen's sad eyes study me, and I turn away. She pats my arm. "You take as long as you need. Your morning is completely free."

I nod and tug on Dog's leash. "Time to get you back where you belong."

Dog places a paw on my foot as if to say he belongs with me. I square my shoulders and set off for Blend's patio to search for the man in a blue cap.

We don't run.

Every step of the little paws by my side sends my chest into painful turbulence. No more morning cuddles. No more throwing the tennis ball. No more matching outfits. I take deep breaths in and out and slow my stride, but Blend is not that far away. Maybe the owner will need a minute to find parking?

I turn the corner and spot a guy in a blue hat at a table on the patio. Either Dog doesn't see him or is not interested because Dog pays no attention. His eyes are on me. My spine stiffens as I falter. Any minute now, Dog will see his owner, and this will be over.

My throat swells. Gretchen was right. I tighten my grip on the leash. I'm going to miss this little guy. How is it possible to have grown attached to him in just a month? His owner will have to come over to the office to pick up the stuff Gretchen purchased. Maybe he'll need dog-sitting services. Maybe I can have Dog during the day. Shared custody?

I stop in my tracks.

What I really want is to put Dog in my truck and drive in the opposite direction. My heart seizes. What is this clawing feeling below my ribs? I cough and pound my chest, but it only grows tighter. How did Dog get loose anyhow? I grind my teeth. Is this man an irresponsible owner? I should ask for his ID and run a background check on him before I hand Dog over.

"Hi." The man rises from his seat. His wide grin sickens my stomach. "Rocko." He surges forward. "I've missed . . . oh." The glean in his eyes dims as it lands on Dog.

"Something wrong?"

The man sighs. "That's not Rocko."

My grip on the leash loosens as I look between the man and my dog.

My dog . . .

That's exactly what Dog has become. Maybe I haven't been fully ready to admit that until this very moment. I feel for the guy, but I'm also filled with so much relief.

"I'm sorry," I tell the stranger as I hide my smile.

"So am I," the man says with a sad nod.

"I hope you find him." I shake his hand.

Waving to the retreating figure, I gently tug on Dog's leash and enter Blend, the coffee shop I haven't been to since Dog arrived. I take a deep breath. Even the aroma of bitter espresso smells sweet like sugar.

"Welcome back." The barista behind the bar grins. "The usual?"

"Please."

"Is that everything?"

It's such a beautiful day that I think I should treat myself. Yep. I deserve this.

"One cupcake." I peruse the selection. "Caramel." Something else catches my eye. "Are those dog biscuits?"

The barista opens the container. "They are. It's a new product we're trying out."

"Two of those as well."

I pay for my order and head to the end of the counter.

"One black coffee, a caramel cupcake, and two dog biscuits." The barista slides my order across the counter. "Pablo!" The barista bends down and tickles the dog at the base of his tail. The dog spins in circles like he's found his favorite person.

My shoulders tense, my newfound relief vanishing. "He recognizes you."

"Smart dog."

"Yes, he is." I rub behind Pablo's ear. He places two paws on my thigh and gives me an "i-told-you-so" grin followed by a lick on my cheek. "How do you know him?"

"He used to be Felix's."

Pablo's ears go stick-straight. His tail pops up and starts wagging really fast. He stands at alert, looking all around the coffee shop as if searching for someone.

The barista frowns. "I was wondering what happened to Pablo when I heard about Felix passing away a few weeks back. Sudden heart attack."

The boulder in my throat returns. I crouch down and pat the scruffy fur on the dog's head.

"They used to come to work together at the storefront you're in now. Even after Felix retired last year, they would come to the park down the road and here for coffee afterward. The dog biscuits were Felix's idea."

Pablo yelps and gives a whimpering howl.

My lungs constrict.

"Glad he found a new home with you, Sven."

I open my mouth to correct the barista, but another customer enters the coffee shop, and he directs his attention to them.

Pablo deflates to the ground. A pitiful howl breaks out of his tiny body. He stares into my eyes and waits. If he weren't a dog, I'd say he was crying.

"Come here." I wrap my arms around the shivering body and stand. He curls into me and puts his head on my shoulder. I bring our foreheads together and his wet nose touches mine. "Let's find us a seat."

At the nearest empty table, I slump into the chair. Pablo slides onto my lap. I pet his fur until his heart rate slows under my palm. His tail gives a hesitant wag. He sits up and looks at me, waiting. I offer him one of the biscuits.

Pablo snaps it up, crunching away. I take a bite of my cupcake. He jumps off my lap, circles around my feet, and puts his head on my shoes. We sit and watch the people buzz in and out, unaware that today is not like any other day. The warmth from the coffee spreads through my body.

Today, Pablo is mine. And I am his.

I take a deep, leisurely breath in and peer down at my companion. "What do you say, Pablo? Shall we go home?"

We exit Blend and step into a bright, sunny winter morning.

Pablo leads the way, and I happily follow.

EIGHT

Dog

My head hangs out of Beast's, I mean, Sven's truck. The wind feels fantastic in my fur even though my eyes are so dry I have to keep blinking. But I can't *not* do it. This has been a much longer drive than when Dad used to take me to drive-thrus for chicken nuggets. Apart from the coffee shop, Sven hasn't visited any of Dad's favorite food places. It's been kibble with an occasional treat. I feel like I'm withering away. But I can run faster, so at least there's that. I lick my muzzle. Good thing I still have my bone. I give a wink to my girl, proudly displayed on the seat next to me. I could almost smile if it weren't for Sven side-eyeing me like he's going to drop me off at the vet.

The car stops. I yip at him. I don't like the vet.

"Do you want to go for a walk?" Sven asks.

Walks are my second favorite thing after my bone. No, third. Because Dad is my most favorite thing. My ears perk up. I run across the seat onto Sven's lap and back to my window. Sven is now, for sure, number two after Dad. Okay, walks are fourth. How can I say no to a walk with Sven? I perk up and grab my bone in my teeth. My butt wiggles so fast I think it'll fly off.

Hopefully, chicken nuggets are still involved.

I jump down from the car, grinning behind my bone. It isn't a drive-thru or a vet. There are trees and grass, but it's also not a park. The acrid smell of gunpowder hangs in the air. This smells like the other place where Dad and I said goodbye to our Marine friends.

My ears lower, and a heavy sadness creeps through me. I start to shake, and my tail hides between my legs. Who are we here to say goodbye to?

Every time we came, there was that part when they would lower the box and then . . . the loud booms. At first, the noise scared me. I wanted to run. The air reeked. But after several visits, I learned what those smells and sounds meant.

When dogs go for a long nap, the one they never wake up from, their scent changes. The scent from the booms meant that the Marine wouldn't wake up either. It was the humans' way of saying goodbye.

"Komm hier." Sven steps are heavier than usual.

I trot after him. His face is unreadable. By now, I know most of Sven's expressions. This is a new one. He's not exactly grumpy like when he gets interrupted or put out like when he scoops up my poops. Sven's nostrils flare like mine do when I'm trying to sniff my way around. I bump my head against his calf and woof, "Are you okay?"

Sven stops and bends down, patting his leg. We're by a fresh mound of dirt. I creep up to him, tuck my tail low, press my ears back, and sit as close to him as possible.

"I found your owner, Pablo." Sven's gentle rubs to my head are as soft as his voice.

Owner? *My* owner?

My dad?

Did Sven find Dad?

"Felix . . . your dad . . . he's gone. He died." Sven pauses and looks at me.

An understanding passes between us. I drop my bone at Sven's feet and paw his hand. Are those tears I see in his eyes?

"This . . ." he turns back to the fresh dirt, "is where we say goodbye."

From his pocket, Sven pulls out the white hat Dad wore. I sniff it, and my heart bursts with pain. I know that scent. Dad. In the distance, the same gunshots we used to hear at all the funerals go off. The smell of gunpowder fills my nose. I look from Sven to the dirt. I sniff and dig a little, searching for a stronger scent, but I can't find one. I don't understand everything, but I know this spot is important.

It clicks in my head.

Dad isn't coming back.

Dad's dead.

I whimper a soft goodbye and drop my head.

My nose touches my bone, the only thing of Dad's I have left. He got it for me because I was his goodest boy. I nudge my bone. Dad has always been my goodest boy. I will never forget our days training to sniff bombs, the years of finding the bad guys, and the memories of serving our country together. The retirement life was different. My heart warms at the memory of Dad throwing the tennis ball for me in the park. I loved our car rides for dinner and our morning walks to the coffee shop. But also our quiet days in the office when Dad spent too much time on his poop pot while I hid my bone.

I lay my bone on the dirt, raise my snout to the sky, and howl.

Booms fill my ears. One. Two. Each thunders inside my body, competing with my cries. A third echo, and then there's nothing. I stop. The sudden silence is so quiet I can hear my heart breaking.

A heart that will never stop loving Dad.

I straighten and sit at attention with my chest out. As a final salute, I give Dad the moment of silence he deserves.

Beside me, Sven sniffs.

His hand reaches over, and he places Dad's hat next to my bone.

Our gazes meet. Eyes glassy, Sven hoists me into the air, stands tall, and gives his salute. Marine to Marine. My body relaxes, and I nestle into the crook of his arm. The hard line of Sven's jaw slackens.

"I don't know for sure." His voice trembles. A tear runs down his cheek. "But maybe your dad led you to the office to find me."

"You might be right, Sven," I woof and lick the tear off his face. This is what Dad would've wanted. He *did* train me to find what's important. I paw at Sven's chest. That *must* be you. My ears perk up. I got it! I know what my new job should be.

Looking after you.

You really have been a good friend. You always make sure I have enough food. You never complain about our necessary seven daily outside trips. And I even like the sweaters Gretchen insists I wear. Plus, you're getting real good at throwing that tennis ball.

"You're going to be okay." He wraps his arms around me.

I rest my head on his shoulder. Our hearts beat in sync.

"You'll never be alone again," he says.

I wag my tail as hard as I can. You won't be alone either, buddy.

"I can't replace your dad, but if you'd like, Pablo, we can be forever roommates." He swallows hard.

Is that how he asks the ladies out on a date? I'm adding that to the list of what I'll need to help him with.

Time for a new list.

Get Sven to smile. Get chicken nuggets. Get Sven a lady-friend. Get me a new bone.

I stare into Sven's eyes. Ready to tackle item number one, I grin. His lips twitch. I smile bigger, my tongue dripping slobber on his jacket. He shakes his head. I'm so close, I can finish this list by tonight. I bark with excitement. A smile splits Sven's face.

All of his teeth are on display.

Damn, I'm good.

Maybe I can convince my new roomie to stop for chicken nuggets on the way home.

Thank you for reading Sven and Pablo's meet cute.

Join our mailing list at willadrew.com for behind the scenes fun, bonus content and upcoming books, including Sven's full length romance book

Ooh and as a special treat, next is a sneak peak of WE Blend, featuring Sven.

WE Blend by Willa Drew Sneak Peek

ONE

Fame follows me everywhere.

Not today. This morning I'm invisible. Everything is going according to plan and twelve hours crammed upright in an airplane seat were a small price to pay for my freedom. London commuters rush by on their way to work as I stroll back to my hotel sipping my average cup of Joe. No bodyguard in sight.

A smattering of paparazzi in front of the marble staircase sends my heart beating faster. No. They can't know I'm here. Can they? I tug the brim of my baseball cap. I look nothing like myself. Maybe I should've picked a smaller hotel, but the Four Seasons is where Dad always stays. Lots of celebrities choose it.

I rush past the cameras and try not to groan at how long the doorman takes to open the wrought iron doors. Inside the hotel, it's quiet and calm. Made it.

"Melodie." I hear my name ring across the gleaming two-story lobby.

A shiver shoots up my spine. "Dad?"

I look over to the plush maroon couches arranged in a semi-circle, and sure enough, there's Bill Rockerby. Stepdad to me. Rocker to the world. That's who the press is here for. He's not even hiding his rockstar status, decked out in black leather like he just walked off the stage after one of his concerts. Except he's walking toward me, his mouth pressed into a thin line, the look of disappointment I dread souring the handsome face lots of women, and men, drool over.

"What are you doing here?" I stumble over my words.

"The better question is, what are you doing here?" His voice is low and tense.

"I—" I don't have a comeback. Truth: I'm supposed to be in New York on a shopping spree, chaperoned by my mother-approved cousins, not in this swanky hotel in London.

His hand is on my arm. "Not here." Amber eyes dart left and right and back again. "People are listening." Dad's always paranoid about the press, especially in Europe. He corrals me toward the elevator, presses the call button, and we stand in awkward silence as we wait.

My mind races between two thoughts. Was it Bailey or Zoe who spilled the beans? 'Cause they were supposed to cover for me and not fold less than twenty-four hours into my escape. We have a pact: provide alibis for each other when we need to escape the parental cages, but their end of the bargain is harder to uphold. And I've never left the country by myself before. Zoe asked me five times if I was sure about the ruse.

More important: How do I get out of this?

There's a soft ding, probably a D-flat but the pitch is off a hair, and the gold doors slide open. I jump in first, hit the button for my floor; Dad follows close behind. More silence, like the pause between songs on a playlist. The doors close, and the elevator jumps to life.

"Your mother is sick with worry."

Slash. His words are tiny shavings of metal cutting at me. He knows my weak spot. Making Mom anxious, given what she's going through, is one of the worst things I could do. I squeeze my teeth together and don't reply because I've never learned to lie. My parents' publicist keeps trying to coach me, but the closest I can get is to omit the truth. Ask me a direct question, and

I'll blabber, but I can't tell Dad about why I'm here.

"You can't silence your way out of this mess. Is it Dillon? I called him as soon as your mother got the alert on her credit card about the hotel charge." The elevator is playing a Muzak version of Justin's *Holy*, and my ears want to bleed. "He pretended he hadn't heard from you—better at lying than your cousins."

Mom's card. The receptionist said they had to have one in case I have other charges but promised they won't use it as long as I pay cash. Months of saved allowance was just enough for a ticket, three nights at the hotel, food, and paying for recording my music video. I'm not staying at this chain anymore. All the talk about keeping their clients' confidentiality, and they sell me out to my parents within hours.

"Talk to me." His voice softens a bit, and he angles his body toward me. "I might be forty-two, but I remember what being young and in love was like. I thought you were over him. With him back in England, you stopped pining for the asshole, pardon my French."

Dillon. Right. If I agree I'm here for Dillon, Dad might not dig deeper. My plan might still have a chance. "I thought I loved Dillon." It's true. I did think that. I don't anymore, but I let Dad draw his own conclusions. I keep squeezing my teeth. I can do it. Don't say anything, don't say anything, don't say anything.

"And what was your thought process? Fly across the ocean, profess your love for him, and hope, what? That he'll ditch his new job and come back to the States for you?"

New job? Is that why he left? He didn't offer me an explanation when he sent me his "I'm sorry, I can't do this" text.

I don't trust myself to speak, so I shrug instead.

"It's been six months."

The elevator doors open, and I trudge to my room, push the heavy door, and sink onto the king-size bed, leaving the chair by the desk for

Dad to sit in. The calm gray-blue hues of the room cool the emotions circulating between us.

"You know you don't have to lie."

I want to scream "I do. You won't let me do anything otherwise."

"You know we love you."

"I know." This one's no lie. If anything, they love me too much. So much, there's no room for anything else.

"And that we do these things to protect your privacy. To keep you safe from another paparazzi-triggered breakdown. Can you blame your mother for wanting a semblance of normalcy for you?"

"Nope." After what happened to Papa and me, I can never blame her for wanting to keep me safe. But I don't have to like it. The bubble-wrapped life is smothering me. Sometimes I feel like I can't breathe between the rules, the bodyguards, and the ever-narrowing circle of things to do or people to do them with. Probably not a good time to bring up my complaints.

Today, I need all suspicion away from the true reason I'm in London. And it isn't Dillon.

"I'll call your mom while you pack, tell her you're safe. The pilot's getting the jet ready for us."

"But . . ." If I don't show up to my meeting with Mr. Astor tomorrow, I'll lose the fifty percent down payment I transferred. "Can I at least go talk to Dillon?" I run my hand through my hair, find the familiar strands that always feel different, out of place, and pull, causing just enough pain to distract me from spilling the truth. The pain merges with the cloud of cutting metal of Dad's words.

"Why do you want to go down that road?" Dad puts his Doc Martin on his knee and shakes his foot. "No. You're not leaving this room until I escort you to the plane. It's nonnegotiable."

"But, Dad—"

"Melodie." He touches my hand, and I stop with the hair.

I focus on my tennis shoes and not on the buzzing shrapnel in my chest.

"Look at me."

I do as he says, because I'm a good girl.

"Leave it be."

Damn. There is no getting out of this. I'll have to message Lenard Astor and figure out a way, another time we can find two days in his schedule. Even if I do lose part of the money, I'll make it up with several months' of my allowance, if I buy nothing at all.

"Oh, and since you insist on being treated like an adult, it's time you took on some adult responsibilities. How about getting a job?"

"This again. I don't even have a high school diploma. How would it look if your stepdaughter asks 'do you want fries with that' for a living?"

"I wouldn't mind as long as you're happy."

He always says stuff like this. Cares almost too much. Unlike Mom who loves me but uses the tough-love parenting style. Nice or not, my music is my priority. "How can I be happy doing that when what I'd make at such a place is pennies compared to my allowance."

"Your mother wants to cut off your allowance as well."

"She can't. I have expenses." The metal ball of doom swings on a chain, and I cling to it, not wanting to wreck my plans.

"Really?" His bushy eyebrow performs that sky high thing it does when he's being sarcastic. "We pay for everything."

"I need clothes."

"You have two walk-in closets."

"I was going to buy a new keyboard."

"What's wrong with the one in the studio?"

"That's yours."

"I have a solution. Why don't you come and work for me at Rocker, Inc. Nadine needs help in the back office. It'll give you some work experience and you can help discover the next *it* artist."

I don't want to discover them, I want to *be* them. But I need the money to start again, and working for my stepfather isn't the worst thing in the world. "What's the starting salary?"

He smiles for the first time. "You make it sound like you're doing me a favor here and not the reverse. I'll pay you the same as I'd pay anyone I'd hire to do the job. And no special treatment. You'll be like any of my other employees."

It's not as if I have a lot of choice here. "Fine."

I grab the suitcase Mom gave me for my eighteenth birthday and fling the lid open. I stuff the ten outfits I brought for my stay into it and hide my sheet music under the top dress. My independence day's gone. Guess it's back to the US for the Fourth of July.

"This is ridiculous." The bright yellow Louis Vuitton with my initials monogrammed in blue, MVR for Melodie Vella Rockerby, mocks my ruined dreams with its bright cheer.

"You running away is what's ridiculous." His phone dings an F-sharp, and he answers.

"Yes. I'm with her. Yes. Safe." I can feel his eyes on my back as I snap my suitcase shut. "I told her the terms. Love you too."

He puts the phone down and gets up. "I have to go make an excuse to the press. They spotted me at Southend when I landed. Wait for me here. Hotel security has someone by your door. Don't even try talking to them."

The lead ball drops from my chest into my stomach at the sight of the security guard when Dad leaves my room. I grab onto the doorframe and take a moment to survey the hallway, looking for possible escape routes.

"Get inside and stay there." Patience is no longer in Dad's voice, and I want to scream. Instead, I slam the door.

The heavy metal doesn't connect but bounces off the fingers on my left hand, still clutching the white casing. I jerk them toward me and watch the indentations on the index and middle finger bloom pink. At the sight, the numbness disappears, replaced by blinding pain. The scream I've wished for erupts from my lungs. I suck air and glare at the places where the edge of the door tore through the skin. It doesn't look that bad. That's when the throbbing begins, and I can barely hear Dad barking orders at the guard to get the hotel doctor.

This is not how I imagined my first jail break would go.

TWO

I haven't been in LA for more than five minutes, and he walks right by me. So close, I can
almost smell his designer cologne. A few steps,
and I could slap him on the back, assuming I
could get past the security detail.

My father. The rockstar.

Bill Rockerby strolls through the airport, his
entourage carrying bright yellow luggage like

little ducks in a row, while I stand here at baggage claim waiting for mine like a normal person.

Is that his stepdaughter in the back? She sure lucked out when her mother remarried, getting a rockstar as her new father. Some tossers get all the breaks. She doesn't look happy about being home. One hand sports a splint binding her fingers together. Did Daddy's little girl's vacation get ruined? Poor her. Not.

The sunglasses that hold up her red hair surely cost more than my entire wardrobe. Her signature streak falls on the left side of her face. If not for that shock of white, from this close she looks more like a girl next door than the glossy spoiled brat in the pages of the magazines Mum used to bring home from the clinic. Without the makeup and the posh clothes, her beauty shines. Not my type, but plenty of people would love to have someone like her as their arm candy.

Whispers start around me, and phones turn in their direction. Some brave souls take a few steps to get closer, others shout about getting a selfie. Rocker and Melodie keep walking. We're nothing but an annoyance to them. They could've smiled, waved, but no, not rock-n-roll's elite. They press on with sour faces and disappear from view.

"I almost touched him," a bloke in denim overall shorts and flip-flops gushes to the girl next to him. American fashion is not something I'll ever understand.

I unzip the inside pocket of my GOODBOIS messenger bag, the one nice thing I own, and get out the small notebook covered in black faux leather. With a pop, the pencil snaps out of the elastic holder, and I jot down:

> Annoyance on the clean face of a perfect
> smile on a glossy page
>
> sound of flip-flops on a linoleum floor
>
> Almost. Always almost.

Notebook safely tucked away, I roll up the sleeves of my dark green shirt. Mum's been supplying me with the pocket notebooks ever since I started writing up the ideas that pop into my head on my hands and arms. There's a drawer full of them at home and two more in my pack that, with any luck, is not lost. I shift the beat-up guitar case from my feet and onto my shoulder and walk closer to the conveyor belt.

Time to let Mum know I've arrived. I connect my phone to the free airport Wi-Fi, pull up WhatsApp, and type "I'm here." She'll relay the message to Opa, who doesn't get the whole text-message thing. I can hear my grandfather grumbling, "Why can't you just pick up the phone?" Even though it's midnight in Bremen, I get a barrage of messages back. Mum should be sleeping, she needs it, but I type back some deets.

The LAX Airport Shuttle bus goes to the Transit Center, where I catch the Number 3 Big Blue Bus, which gets me to Westwood for fifty cents. My kind of price. I get off and make sure my backpack doesn't hit anyone when I turn—the top part is higher than my head, and

I'm taller than most men around me. A short walk, and I arrive at the UCLA campus. It has people, but it's quiet, unlike the one I just left. Had to bail on the rest of the semester for this, but I'll be back in time for the October session.

There are a few people around, and I catch the eye of two beauties lying on a blanket on the grass. They both smile at me, and I make sure to return the gesture. I may be here for serious business, but that doesn't mean a fella can't have fun in the process.

Part of me can't believe my luck in getting into the program. I applied to the Starlight Future Filmmakers Foundation's annual film competition as a laugh. I never thought I'd get a call for the audition. The committee gave me the option to fly in or do it over Zoom. Yeah, 'cause I have the dough to drop on a trip to LA for a bloody interview. Harder to turn on my charm over the internet, but I made it work, and here I am—an almost-all-expenses-paid trip to the U.S. of A.

Checking in to the dorms is the simplest thing I've done today. Let the free ride begin. After the airfare, the credit card I usually only use for emergencies is almost at its limit. Finding a job will be one of the first things on my list. I stick my key into the door but before I turn it, the pale wood slat opens, and a bloke with a buzz cut smiles at me.

"Welcome, bienvenidos, bienvenue—all the languages I know."

"Willkommen," I say.

"Ah, isn't that what they say in Germany?"

"Yup. Born and bred there, so I can vouch for that."

"More of us internationals." He scratches his head. "What's with the British accent?"

"That's ten years learning English at school in Bremen plus summers with family in Sussex."

"Willkommen then, Mr. German."

"It's Wil Peters actually."

"I'm Mateo. Mateo Gallardo." He opens his arms and steps away, so I can enter. The common room isn't a fancy resort, but the light is good, and we're far away from the stairwell. In the middle there's a pair of brown leather couches separated by a low glass table, dominated by a flat screen TV hanging on the wall. Pushed up against the window is a wooden table with six matching chairs. Home sweet home.

"You're the last to arrive, so the only bed left is in my room." He points to the second door on the left. "Me and the other dudes were about to head out and grab some grub. Wanna join?"

I want to drop my stuff and take a shower, but some food wouldn't be bad either. "Sure. Any idea where I can get a SIM card around campus?"

"I'm your man. I scouted all the things we're going to need in this country."

"Including a grocery store? The website said there's a kitchen I can use on this floor." I've learned over the last year living on campus how much Mum did for me. First time I did laundry, I washed my clothes in one load. I still have the shirt that used to be white and is now a combination of gray and splotches of blue. Cooking is another thing I had to figure out.

"You're ambitious. It's just for three months. One thing my mami never let me do is cooking. I already miss her empanadas."

Mateo shrugs as he follows me into the room we are to share. Why do the people who design dorms lack imagination? They're all the same. Two single beds pushed against opposite walls, one night table, and what I presume is a closet the size of a coffin.

I drop my backpack on the bed and prop my guitar in the small space against the wall.

"You here to make a movie too?" Mateo sits down on his bed.

"Yeah, I'm the sound person."

"Way cool." He taps his chest. "Set designer. I'm on the green team."

"Green?"

"Each team has a color. Don't worry." Why would I worry? "You'll get one at the orientation session tomorrow. We can go together in the morning. Already checked out the building."

Seems my luck is holding. Mateo is doing the heavy lifting.

I hang up a classic white long-sleeve shirt Mum snuck in that raises the number of clothing items I brought to eleven. My side of the room looks spartan compared to Mateo's, who on his twelve-hour drive from Mexico brought twice the stuff I had in my old dorm room at uni. I'm particularly impressed with the precise placement of the array of multicolored pens and pencils he's using to draw something in a large notepad. He catches me eyeing them.

"Tools of the trade. I always sketch by hand first."

Day one in the States rushes by in a blur of dropping more money on my credit card. I thought the giant Coke I drank with my first American burger would keep me up but incessant yawning reminds me I've been awake for twenty-four hours.

When I get back from the shower, the bedroom is empty and quiet but for the laughter filtering from the living room where my new flatmates are gearing up to play a video game. I set my alarm for five a.m. so I can fit in a quick workout before orientation. The gym on campus even has rowing machines, so I can keep up with my crew in Berlin. They'll be rowing on the river daily. Can't get out of shape.

Exhaustion seeps out of me into the mattress, and I stare at the curtains filtering thin pinpoints of light through the top. I'm here. If Opa's right, I'll figure out a way to meet Rocker. I've come the farthest I've ever been from home to talk to the man. And for Mum, I'd go around the world in a rowing boat to improve her health.

The rockstar can spare the money, go without another car or a house in Fiji. It's not like he had to pay child support for eighteen years. What I need is a fraction of what that would've cost him. I'm not looking for a father. Opa filled those shoes for me, but Rocker should help.

Mum's done everything for me, her only son. Even if I am just the product of a one-night stand, I'm the only blood offspring that wanker has in this world, and I'm ready to use that fact.

I'm not going home empty-handed.

THREE

The dang splint protecting my injured fingers gets stuck in the sleeve of my turquoise dress shirt, and I have to rethink my outfit. No sleeves. I move the hangers in the silver section around until I spot the vintage Paco Rabanne metal chain halter I kept after the *Rock Squad Magazine* photoshoot for Dad's kids charity fundraiser. The cold links were my armor against the photographer's words telling me where I should stand and what my face should look like. I hang it back up. That is Melodie Rockerby's outfit, not El Vella's.

What will El wear? My stage name is my nod to Papa. Technically, it's still my name, the Rockerby added when Mom married Bill Rockerby. He sat me down and asked if I was okay with him adopting me, explained he never had any kids of his own, would never replace Papa, but he wanted us to be a family. It's not like I could say no. True to his word, Bill, Dad, has always treated me like his, and I do love him. I know I'm lucky, but Rockerby is too famous, too recognizable. No one outside of the opera world will know the last name Vella, which is perfect. I need them to see *me*.

I tuck my hair behind my ear. What would I wear if I didn't have to think about the tabloids and eventual comments on social media? Something comfortable, because tonight's gonna be tough enough without having to worry about my clothes; something I can keep my cool in, because I'll be sweating all over; something I can sit down in without worrying about showing my underwear.

My last vacation in Malta with Papa's family, I went shopping at the local market and got the most comfortable moss-green palazzo pants that sorta looked like a long skirt, along with a simple white tank top. My arms glide through the holes and my heartrate slows a bit. Memories of the sun and the simple conversations envelop me, offering support. There's something about clothes that sets my mood, and I've found the right ones for El Vella's first stage appearance.

"Are you ready?" Sven asks from behind the closed door. "We have to leave in five." My friend is less than pleased with me since Dad reassigned him from lead bodyguard duty to my personal babysitter. I lucked out, though. If Dad only knew the messes Sven cleaned up for me. There's no one I'd rather have by my side day and night.

Am I really doing it? Stepping on a stage, however small, and not fainting from the greedy eyes trained on me, ready to judge my every wrong word, false pitch, awkward movement? My hands shake when I open the door and follow Sven down the stairs, panting a little too hard. Not good signs, but I have to ignore them. We sneak past the theater room where Mom and Dad are binge watching some historical drama about a queen.

"And where are you going?" Mom's voice stops me in my tracks. I'll need a better route next time.

"Ice cream with Zoe." I've already texted my cousin to cover if my parents get nosey.

"And Sven?" Mom turns around and sees my human shield looming behind me. "Be home by midnight."

I hurry down the hallway before she changes her mind.

Sven opens the back door of the light blue electric Rolls Royce Dad got for my required bodyguard to chauffeur me around, and I slip in. The door clicks shut, surrounding me in silence. Almost. My ears are ringing. My personal Superman jumps in and starts driving us to downtown LA.

Outside the tinted windows, the sky deepens into a purple haze as day morphs into night. Time for my transformation as well. I pull out my phone and follow the instructions on the YouTube video I've watched a hundred times. I finagle my shoulder-length auburn hair into flat twists and cover them with a wig. The platinum locks are longer than my real hair and feel odd falling over my shoulders and down my back to my waist. A little shine on my lips completes the look.

"You are not allowed to go into the actual bar." Sven repeats the instructions he gave me twice before, ignoring my new look. "All the performers under twenty-one have to stay backstage."

"I know."

"I've checked out the place, and I'll be in the back, the left corner closest to the hallway that leads backstage. It'll take me maybe thirty seconds to get to you if you are recognized."

"Left back corner. I got it."

"And you're not talking to anyone but me and Pauline, the manager. You're there to get that job, not have fun at a bar."

"Aye, aye, captain."

"Not funny, Melodie. You don't have to do this. We can turn around and go home." He stops at the red light and looks over his shoulder at me. "There are other ways to get money. Let me help you for once. I'll get a loan and give you the cash, and you'll pay me back once Mr. and Mrs. Rockerby reinstate your allowance."

"Which, according to Mom, is never."

"They're still angry. Give them time."

"I'm angry too."

Sven does his silent listening routine.

"If I'm doing it, and dammit, I am doing it, I'm doing it on my own. I'm not the useless, spoiled baby they think I am. I might not have a formal education"—I air quote the words—"but I had the world's best tutors. Taking the GED seemed more trouble than it was worth. Not like university has ever been in the picture." I sit up straighter, raise my chin, and meet Sven's eyes in the rearview mirror. "But I know a lot about music, and I can earn my own money, live my own life, and be my own person. I don't need them as much as they think I do."

Even though I booked Mr. Astor's last available session in November, my down payment is gone, and the salary at Rocker, Inc. is a start but it's not going to get me the amount I need to cover the cost. Zoe felt bad about the London debacle and offered to make up the difference. After I refused to accept her money, she pulled some strings and snagged me a spot in tonight's open mic competition. The winner gets paid to perform at the Devil's Martini's coveted Saturday night showcase.

This gig alone won't cover the whole sum, but it'll make a big dent. If my plan is to become a singer, why not start now? I've spent enough hours practicing in my room and Dad's home studio to stand a chance. If I win, I prove to everyone I can earn a living with my music.

We enter through a side door of the Devil's Martini, and a preppy young woman in glasses, who looks more like a librarian than someone who'd work at a bar, shoves a clipboard my way.

"Write your name here. You're number five." She hands me a sticker with the number hand-written in red marker. "Are you performing too? Or just the boyfriend?" Her eyes survey Sven's solid body from head to foot, and I swear the top of her cheeks pink up.

"Friend. Audience." Sven gives his standard just-the-facts reply.

"Oh, straight through there, then." Her cheeks are definitely pink when she shows my fair-haired "friend" the way. "And you go left." She switches to me. "You get one song. Hang around till the end, Pauline'll talk to you about the gig if you win. And don't try to butter me up, I'm not one of the judges. Break a leg."

The door slams behind me. She glances at Sven one more time and aims her smile at the next person. We head past her, and I take the door to the left that says, "STAGE. STAFF ONLY," and Sven gives me a thumbs up as he heads up the long hallway and into the bar. I wipe my sweaty palms on the sleek silk crepe of my pants.

The stage is my friend. The stage is my friend.

I'll get on it even if I have to ask someone to push me out. Recording a video for my EP won't happen if I can't perform in front of a crowd. Doubt this dinky bar will even have more than twenty people here, but as long as it's more than zero, it won't be easy.

I knew this day was coming. I just didn't expect it to be this soon. I thought I'd have time. Shoot the video, send it to some producers, make a whole album before I had to perform in front of real live people.

Twenty minutes later, the open mic competition begins, and Jeremiah is not here. My feverish texts go unanswered, and although they have an extra keyboard and a couple of guitars I could use, my broken fingers will take at least five more weeks before I can start using them again. This is what Jeremiah is for: study the music for my songs, bring a guitar, and accompany me. Now what do I do?

I walk up the hallway to the bar area, peek from the door into the room, and scan the place. Jeremiah is steps away, beer in hand, sitting at a dark wooden bar talking with some guy. That jerk. He shouldn't be drinking before we perform. He should be backstage rehearsing, or at least have the decency to answer his phone. I'm not letting him screw this up for me. Google informed me both Dasher and Carlee Waters had their break after winning the open mic competition here. Maybe El Vella can be next.

"Jeremiah," I shout across the room. "Jeremiah, over here."

Jeremiah looks up and meets my eye. My breath hitches. He can barely focus on me. How much has this dufus had to drink? I look at my phone. Our slot is in ten minutes. How can I sober him up? I look for Sven, but he's far off, the librarian's hand on his impressive bicep and his attention on her blazing cheeks and not the bar I'm not even supposed to be in. I don't need him to show up, scare Jeremiah, and end this night before I even get a chance. One eye on Sven, I slink over the black floor to Jeremiah's barstool.

"Jeremiah?" The way his body sways when he moves his head kills any hope of him being my hands today.

"Ellllllll." The happy drunk sings my name. I could kill him. He's no use to me in this state. I side-eye his companion who's drinking . . . water? Odd.

"Meet my new friend. He'sss from Germany. How cooool is that?"

I don't have time to meet people. I need Jeremiah to sober up. I don't have a choice.

"Hey, I'm Wil." I turn to him because my parents taught me manners. His one-sided grin is certain to score, but it's not going to work on me. I'm here on a mission, and it's not a random hook-up with a hot stranger. This is the one time I wish Sven were by my side, so I could get him to remove this playboy. I flick my gaze to Sven to reassure myself he's there and if I scream his name, he'll run over and rescue me.

"Hey. Um, can I talk to Jeremiah? In private."

Light brown, almost golden eyes examine my outfit, the ends of my hair sweeping my hip bones, the exposed skin at my neck, and finishes the round with my face. If I weren't already hot from nerves, that stare would've gotten me there. He's cute, jet-black hair flopping all over the place in that boy-band-wannabe way. He reminds me of someone, but I can't quite put my finger on whom. I shake my head. I have bigger problems.

"Could you please give us some space?" I take one step closer, as if I can intimidate him into vacating his spot.

"Not sure it's smart for you to be next to him before your turn on stage." Wil nods at the number five sticker on my shoulder. His accent is decidedly British. Didn't Jeremiah say this dude was from Germany? Or is Jeremiah too drunk to know the difference between the two countries? "He might just chuck up all over your pretty clothes and ruin your performance before you begin. How about I keep an eye on your boyfriend, and you can talk it out after you're done?"

"No."

"No?" His thick dark eyebrow climbs up, and a smile returns to his face. Maybe it is working on me. Would've worked if I didn't have a drunk Jeremiah and my dreams riding on the line.

"No. He's not my boyfriend. Who has time for that?" Why am I telling him I'm single? Need to focus. "I hired him to play the guitar for me." I raise my splinted fingers and shove them in front of Wil's face. "See?"

"Well, that clears that."

If I expected sympathy from this dude, I didn't get it.

"I don't do the girlfriend thing either. Not planning on starting it now." He licks his lips like I might be his next meal. "Jeremiah might have difficulty standing up, so playing an instrument is bloody unlikely."

"Dammit." I know the guy is right.

We both turn to regard the hoodie-clad Jeremiah, currently staring into his half-empty beer glass as if the golden liquid has the answers to every mystery in life.

"What did you say your name was?" Wil's molten stare focuses on my eyes then my mouth, as if he were ready to catch whatever tumbles out next. And I wish I were here for fun. Hot, kiss-worthy fun.

"El. El Vella." My voice sounds raspier than normal.

His eyes flash back to mine. Something switches in them. He re-surveys me, and his demeanor changes. The relaxed flirty vibe drops as fast as the last note of Dad's latest hit. He loses his smile, the fire in his eyes gone, and for reasons I can't understand, I miss it already.

Wil leans in like he's going to kiss me, his fiery breath tickling my ear instead. Is this his signature move? Is he going to ask me out? Would I say yes? Goosebumps run down my arms, and my heart rises to my throat.

"I know who you are."

END OF SNEAK PEEK

FALLING FOR THE ROCKSTAR'S DAUGHTER

A friends-to-lovers, slow burn romance featuring a reluctant collaboration between two musicians.

WE Blend

WE Breathe

WE Balance

ACKNOWLEDGEMENTS

From Willa Drew

Serendipity is one of the forces that played a role in the creation of this little novella. So many strings had to come together and we're so grateful they did.

Sven, our grumpy bodyguard, started as a minor side character in our *WE Blend* slow-burn romance series and grew into a beloved secondary character as the series progressed. Readers fell for him so much that the members of our Discord reader group even created a "More Sven" command. We always knew that, by the end of the *WE* series, Sven would have his own story and we even had a romantic interest in mind for him.

Pablo, the dog, is heavily inspired by A. Miracle's real-life terrier, also named Pablo, who has his own TikTok channel and is an absolute hoot. Ashley (A. Miracle) first discovered Willa Drew through the Ohio Book Dragons Facebook group and became one of our earliest ARC readers for the *WE* series.

In 2024, during the Beyond the Reader Author Event (BRAE) in Columbus, OH, Ashley visited us and Gala (aka Drew) got to meet the real-life Pablo in person!

As Ashley worked on a book of her own (follow her on Instagram @miraclea_ and TikTok @actuallyamiracle222and Pablo on TikTok @Pablo_toks5), we often talked about the writing process.

Later that fall, after devastating hurricanes struck North Carolina and Florida, author Ariana St. Claire organized an anthology of novellas to benefit pets and their families affected by the storms.

Charity has always been one of Willa Drew's core values. If you've read our other books, you've probably noticed that theme and the various causes our characters support. We had only a couple of months to complete our novella for the anthology, and we didn't want to invent a brand-new cast of characters. Since we had just finished publishing the final *WE* trilogy book and DL (aka Willa) was sad about saying goodbye to Sven for a while, the threads connected beautifully.

We invited A. Miracle to co-write the novella, and *Taming the Grumpy Bodyguard* was born. It was originally published in December 2024 as part of the *Pawliday* charity collection.

That collection is now out of print, but we want to continue supporting charitable causes with this story. All proceeds from *Taming the Grumpy Bodyguard* will go to charities that help pets and their families. Our plan is to tally proceeds quarterly and donate to a different organization each time. We'll share donation updates on our website and newsletter so readers can see the impact you're part of.

This is also our first book to receive an audiobook edition, narrated by **Jack Graves**, whose voice brings Sven and Pablo to life. If you'd like an hour of audio entertainment, you can find it along with signed editions and other special goodies at **willadrew.com/store**.

To keep up with new releases, behind-the-scenes peeks, and more charity updates, follow us on Instagram and TikTok @willadrewauthor.

Huge thanks to our ARC team and Discord readers for your enthusiasm and early feedback. You keep us writing.

For **A. Miracle**: thank you for hopping in on this author journey with us, for sending us Pablo pictures, for staying up way too late writing and editing, and for just being you. Writing this story together reminded us why we love the writer and reader community so much.

To our readers: this story exists because you asked for more Sven. Thank you for supporting us as authors and for supporting the causes that are dear to us. We love having you in our lives,

Thank you

Editor: Jessica Erin

Cover Art: Cupcake_Cat1235

Cover Design & Formatting: A Fabulous Production

From A. Miracle

Pablo is who he is because of his humans, especially his dad. Caleb was our biggest supporter during writing even if it meant he had to share Pablo. We would be lost without him.

Two authors. Two countries. One obsession with love stories.

Willa Drew's contemporary slow-burn romances are full of feels, playful banter, and high-stakes emotions. Their globetrotting characters fight for love as they discover who they are and where they belong.

Willa, a proud Canadian and devoted Leafs hockey fan, and Drew, a Russian-American with a lifelong love of languages, always search for the perfect words to capture heartbreak and connection.

Their books guarantee swoon-worthy kisses and happily ever afters.

Come hang out with them

@willadrewauthor

willadrew.com

A. Miracle is a new author based in the middle of nowhere, Ohio. She has been writing since she could pick up a pen and now, she is ready to make her dreams come true. She has established herself in the book world in ways of helping other authors with their works while using social media to create safe, fun book spaces where people feel heard, respected and loved.

Her writing journey began as a young child writing lyrics to songs or quotes that she found on the internet using grandma's dial up internet. She was always looking for words that could explain what she was going through but never found the exact words she needed. Her work explores the themes of religious trauma, breaking generational curses and true love, captivating readers with the first-person point of view of pain, questions, fear and healing. Planting a mustard seed of hope into each reader's garden.

Keep an eye out for her upcoming novel Sweet, Sweet Clementine. Coming soon!

Check out her IG @miraclea_ or her Tik tok @actuallyamiracle222

Sweet, Sweet Clementine

When August Sutton chooses love over blood money, he sets in motion a chain of dangerous events that threaten everything he holds dear- and only his love for Clementine Wexley might be enough to save them both.

SERIES BY WILLA DREW

SECOND CHANCE BILLIONAIRES

The Second Chance Billionaires series follows five lifelong friends—a grumpy CEO, a charming playboy, a retiring hockey pro, a British aristocrat, and a sci-fi author—from college roommates to billionaire boardrooms as they each get one more shot at love.

Not a Fake Chance – ROSE & ALEK

Not a Second Chance – CALLUM & OLIVIA

BOOK 3 – LINC & ???

BOOK 4 – BLAKE & ???

BOOK 5 – SOREN & ???

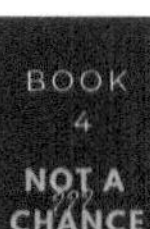

AND US

Watch movies and real life collide with Sarah and Nick in a right person/wrong time, hidden identity, new adult romance. One year, five parts, six major holidays, many twists.

Kisses, Lies, & Us

Passions, Hopes, & Us

Distance, Love, & Us

or binge the complete series with bonus scenes

in

Friendzoned By My Crush

FALLING FOR THE ROCKSTAR'S DAUGHTER

An upper young adult, friends-to-lovers, slow burn romance featuring a reluctant collaboration between two musicians.

WE Blend

WE Breathe

WE Balance

FALLING FOR THE MOVIE STAR

If you like an age gap, brother's best friend romance featuring LA's red-carpet glamor, Irish
charm, and a reunion written in the stars,
Siobhan and Asher's story is for you.
Star Struck

ANDERS INVESTIGATIONS

Meet the men of Anders Investigations, a new contemporary romance series with a romantic suspense element.

Taming the Grumpy Bodyguard

Loving the Grumpy Bodyguard